Cattitude

life-lessons learnt from my cats

Manmohan Singh Dadwal

 pencil

ISBN 978-93-5458-043-7
© Manmohan Singh Dadwal 2021
Published in India 2021 by Pencil

A brand of
One Point Six Technologies Pvt. Ltd.
123, Building J2, Shram Seva Premises,
Wadala Truck Terminal, Wadala (E)
Mumbai 400037, Maharashtra, INDIA
E connect@thepencilapp.com
W www.thepencilapp.com

CONTENTS

About this book

As a kid, I wanted a cat but my mother was understandably against the idea. She knew that she would end up taking care of the cat. I pleaded and cried but my mother did not budge. So I never had a cat and lived perfectly happy without a pet until one day Masala was gifted to us.

Masali was a beauty and had a unique character that inspired us in many ways. At the age of two, she left the world leaving us with her three offsprings: Bali Masala; Garam Masala and Peanut Masala. The three of them will celebrate their first birthday soon- actually we will- cats don't really celebrate birthdays!!

Two years with cats have taught me a lot!! I often look at them for answers. As a self-evaluation tool, I have the masala-crew. I have learnt that cats have a unique wonderful way of living life; a certain verve and nonchalance… a "cattitude"!!

That's what this book is about! Nine lives of Cattitude that I learnt from my cats.

Cattitude is all about Persistance

"It's six am and they are still sleeping!! Humph!!" Bali mutters as he tries to open the window with his paws.His fluffy body hair glowing in the early morning Sun, eyes shining inside the black spots around his eyes. He gives up after a while and begins to sing. It has the desired effect and soon Manu steps out of the bedroom, rubbing his eyes, "good morning Bali" he says and bends down to pick up Bali.

"Oooh c'mon!!" Bali protests, "the bowl!! Am hungry!! Cuddles for later!!"

Manu washes his face and brushes his teeth while Bali continues singing and rubbing himself against his legs. He then fills up the bowl and places it on the front terrace opening into the garden.Bali rushes on to the terrace and within seconds is joined by Garam Masala-who greets Bali with "good morning Bali boy!!"

Bali doesn't lift his head up and replies with, "good morning Garam! Had a night out?"

Garam answers with "Yeah!! I like hanging out in the garden...it's nice and fresh!Plus all the cats are out at night..meet n greet and hangout together, you know!

Besides, my black coat renders me invisible in the dark so it's excellent for hunting."

Bali nods his head in agreement,"Yes!! I agree it is a lovely garden- all those squirrels, mice and birds!! Personally I prefer to cuddle up with Manu and Anika at night; the room is cosy, soft mattresses and air conditioning!!"

"Couldn't wait for me, huh?" Peanut Masala walks in questioning the boys.
"Hey Peenie!!" Bali and Garam greet their sister, "Slept well?"

"Oh yes!!" Peanut replies brushing aside hair from her forehead, "I like my special bed in the corner of the bedroom- it's really nice and comfortable and they always leave the window to my room open so I can come and go as I please!!"

"They are so cute and kind- both of them" all the three cats agree together.

"we are lucky to have staff like them!!", Garam adds as they continue to eat.

The masala-crew finishes off their breakfast and are soon lounging around on the front terrace grooming themselves.

It's seven am when Rose wakes up, freshens up and fixes herself a juice. She finds her chair on the front terrace and immediately Peanut joins her rubbing herself on to her legs. Rose tries to pick up Peanut but she begins to protest. Rose puts her down with a laugh, "little princess touch-me-not…" she looks at Manu and adds, "she doesn't like being picked up, our princess". In the meanwhile,Bali and Garam have come meowing out.Its Balis turn to rub himself against Rose's legs and feet as Garam scratches the wall then begins to go back and forth between Rose and their feeding bowl.

"You fed them, right?" Rose looks at Manu and questions.

"Yes, six am sharp- Bali woke me up as usual" Manu replies with a smile, "they are just trying for that little extra"

Bali continues to rub himself against Rose's legs and Garam jumps onto her lap, singing for food.

"No no no!! You all had food already" she scolds the cats lovingly, "now straight lunch!!"

Rose gets off the chair and grabs a book from the book-shelf on the terrace and is soon busy making notes. Manu is sketching on the couch- he is working on a book about his cats. The cats are sitting around the feeding bowl as if trying to manifest food.

An hour later Peanut is in Manus lap who is still sketching while Garam and Bali now have their attention turned to Manu- both at his feet, singing and tracing the line between Manu and their feeding-bowl. Manu looks at Rose who is busy with her notes, then looks at the cat-circus at his feet, puts down his sheets and pencil and gets off his chair. The cats position themselves near the feeding bowl- they know they have got what they wanted. Manu returns to the terrace with pieces of fish and drops them in the bowl.

Rose looks up at Manu in surprise but decides not to say anything now- it will disrupt her focus.

The cats are happy- they just demonstrated the first law of cattitude:

Always give your best to achieve what you want, it doesn't work, persist till you get what you want.

a true CAT stays focussed

It's nine am and the masala-crew has settled in for a nap in their favourite nooks: Garam on top of the book-shelf, Peanut under the couch and Bali sprawled on it- stretched to max, covering the maximum area of the couch. Rose is still writing. Manu finishes watering the garden and steps on to the terrace. Immediately Garam rushes to his feet and rolls over on his back- that's his demand to be cuddled; his lean body covered with shiny black hair glistening in the morning light.

"Hello Mr.Garam!!" Manu greets him as he bends over and picks up Garam and begins to rub his belly. Garam starts to purr, his head tilted back, tiny paws pointing towards the heavens.It is a tender, peaceful moment filled with Garam's loud purring until a squirrel begins to squeak up in the trees.

Within a second Bali and Garam are at the bottom of the tree, looking up at the squirrel. The squirrel notices the arrival of the cats and stops her descend down the tree and begins to squeak even louder, her tail jumping up and down with every squeak- warning her friends of the arrival of the cats in the garden. The cats wait at the foot of the tree, their eyes constantly on the squirrel: hunting is a game of patience and focus.

An hour later, they seem to abandon the hunt and greet Manu who is filling up their feeding bowl.The cats purr and eat their favourite kitty-treat and stroll into the garden to take up their spots to lounge around. The squirrel, who till now was rooted at the same spot on the tree notices the cats resting and decides that it's safe now and continues her descend down the tree. This would prove to be fatal. She barely manages halfway down the tree when Garam comes flying in the air and grabs her between his teeth. Unnoticed by the squirrel, Garam had spotted the squirrel climbing down and had jumped to the opportunity. Half a second and two leaps later, the squirrel was in his jaws.There was no escape possible!

"Aw!! Poor squirrel!!" says Rose as she looks up at Garam.

"Wow!! What speed!!" says Manu, "not even a second!! I thought they had forgotten about the squirrel and were just chilling in the garden!! Amazing!!"

This was a clear demonstration of the second law of cattitude:
keep a constant eye on your goals- even when relaxing and be ever ready to jump at the opportunity.

The cats spend the next half and hour or so slapping the squirrel around the garden until she cant move anymore.One by one, the masala-crew passes the squirrel around - much like playing football- tossing the dead body up in the air and then grabbing it before it touches the ground.

That's the third law of cattitude:

Celebrate each victory- no matter how tiny!

Celebrating victories with your team strengthens the bond between the team members and helps one appreciate the hard work and skills needed for the victory.It also fills you up with enthusiasm for the next mission.

a true CAT is always well-groomed

By eleven am all that remains of the squirrel are a few tufts of hair. Peanut has retreated to her bed in the room, Bali is sleeping on the porch wall and Garam is under the couch in the front porch.

"Hmmm...heh heh" Garam chuckles to himself as he licks his front paws, "the squirrel- she thought i was not looking!! Heh heh.. Delicious little things! I should focus more on the squirrels...so many of them in the garden!!" he smiles as he focuses his attention on the hind paws licking each finger thoroughly- the cracks between each digit and under the paws. Bali joins Garam under the couch and gets busy doing the same: first the paws get cleant, then the legs and finally both the sides of the body. The both of them then begin to lick clean each other's head, the back of the neck, top of the head and under the chin...all finally clean and shiny!!

The fourth law of cattitude is about grooming:
Cleanliness is next to godliness; a cat is always well-groomed.A cat spends a considerable time of the day cleaning and grooming; afterall, how you look matters when it comes to first impressions of someone.

Grooming done, the cats take time out for a siesta...a few minutes go by when their sleep is broken by the sounds of footsteps. Garam, ever alert, raises his head to see who it is...another cat!! A stranger...an intruder!!

"Hmmm...a stray!! What's she doing here??" Garam wonders as he hisses and takes an aggressive pose: back arched, all his body-hair standing like tiny spikes.

The stranger sees him and stops in her tracks pretending not to notice Garam and sniffs around.,"Aaah!! Food!! Maybe if I am charming enough, they will feed me...after all, they are cat people!!" she wonders, "but what about this guy already posing aggressively? I shall not reciprocate his aggressive stance and approach casually. Let's see what happens"

The stray continues her measured approach to the house when she notices Bali joining Garam, taking a similar stance like his brother.

"Stay away, stranger" Bali hisses, "this is OUR house!!"

The stray continues her approach and just when Bali is about to attack the stranger, Rose notices the stray.

"Look Manu!!" she calls out, "we have a guest!!"

Manu steps out to see who it is.

"isn't she cute?" she asks Manu and is met with a weak

"yeah…"

Manu knows completely well that this cat will be adopted. Garam senses Manu's hesitation and positions himself between Manu's feet, eyes glaring at the stranger.

Rose picks up the stray and begins to wonder what could be her name, "you don't even have a necklace little one!! Are you alone and abandoned?" she asks the stray cat now purring in her arms. "Look Manu, she's purring!! Friendly one...looks like she is homeless.what shall we call her??" she wonders…."Jeera!! We shall call her Jeera Masala!!" Rose is always happy to recall a few words in Hindi that she has picked up.

The stray jumps off Rose's arms and positions herself between her feet. Garam and Bali instantly approach the stranger hissing, "Go away stranger!! This is OUR house!! OUR folks!!"
Bali stops to hiss and steps forward seemingly curious and friendly towards the stranger and then suddenly slaps the visitor. "This house ain't big enough for the four of us!! OUR house!! OUR folks!! You are an outsider...you can't come in here!!"

Rose immediately picks up Jeera and turns to Manu, "get her some food, she seems to be hungry"

A few minutes later Jeera Masala is eating from the kitty bowl while Rose makes sure Garam and Bali don't attack her. Peanut Masala, watching the action from a distance, now steps forward to the bowl hesitatingly and begins to eat alongside Jeera.

"See!!" Rose looks at Manu, Garam and Bali "Peanut has already accepted her!! Now you boys too better accept her as the new member of the masala crew!!"

Bali and Garam retreat under the couch and stare angrily at the newcomer. "Hmph!! Now she's eating from OUR bowl!! Not fair!! Not at all fair!!" both the brothers say in unison.

"So you have a name for her?" Rose turns around to Manu and asks.

 Manu gives a sheepish smile and demands, "you sure we need another cat?? I mean… am already living with four cats: Bali, Garam, Peanut and you!!"

"Oooh Manu!! Look how cute she is!! She is so friendly and doesn't seem to have a home!!" Rose responds."I want to adopt her!!"
"Ok!!!" Manu throws up his hands in the air. "So what name did you have in mind?" he asks Rose who replies with a big smile, "Jeera!! Jeera Masala!!"

The bowl empty, Jeera Masala proceeds to lounge under the table on the porch as Bali and Garam continue to glare at her.

"Hmph!! Lets see if you can enter our house!!" Garam hisses at Jeera. .

Jeera lounges around for a while and then walks away into the garden. "Nice folks," she says to herself, "friendly and kind...I can adopt this house....if only I can get around the two boys…anyway, for now I have a pad of my own and can always come around when I need food and cuddles." With that she jumps over the garden wall and vanishes out of sight.

CATtitude is about Empathy

An urgent conference is called in the afternoon. Bali, Garam and Peanut are gathered in the living room while Manu andRoseare resting in the bedroom.

Bali is the first one to speak. "So we have a situation here...this stranger- Jeera they call her. What shall we do about her?"

"I would like to chase her away" Garam replies, "butRoseis already in love with her!!"

He lets out a sigh and continues "the way she was cuddling her!! You saw that!!?? And she even got to eat from the bowl- OUR BOWL!!" he finishes, his eyes red with anger.

"Yes I didn't like that" Bali says. "...I mean cuddle her if you want but feeding her from our-bowl!? I resent that!"

"Yes!!" Garam adds "let's revolt!! Let's make a plan of action to keep this… this Jeera or whatever away from this house!! We must save and protect our home from strangers! If we don't pretty soon she will have a bed next to one of us !! I don't like this!!

Peanut, who was silent all the while now speaks up.

"Boys!! You both are getting agitated over nothing!!" Peanut says with a hint of disdain in her voice. "Always so aggressive!! Ready to fight...man!! She is cool- she just wandered in here looking for food. She has a place of her own with four slaves to serve her!!"

"How do you know?" Bali and Garam look surprised as they ask her.

"Soon she will move in and overtake our place! She already has Anika under her spell." Bali adds "then you will regret it!!"

Peanut raises a paw to silence them and says,"I spoke to her...we had a little chat over a meal- while you both were hissing and showing off your muscles"

Garam and Bali stare at Peanut in surprise as she continues to speak. "Her slaves have gone out and haven't returned since four days- there's a substitute slave coming once a day to feed her but eating just once a day is not enough- that's why she came here looking for food. She has no intention to take over the house and rule over us so relax!! Besides…I need some girl company; you know, sharing beauty tips and stuff..All you boys can talk about is your war-games!!" Peanut rolls up her eyes as she finishes.

"So now you are on her side!!" Bali says, looking shocked."I can't believe this sis!! You are on her side!!"

"Yeah. I don't like that sister!! Remember what mom always said? LA FAMILIA!! We are a family and we stick together! I tell you , soon she will take over and we will be out of the house- homeless and motherless"

"I miss mom!" Bali says "she would have taken care of this!"

"Guys!!" Peanut cuts off both the boys. "Stop dramatizing the whole thing!! I say we wait and watch. From what i know of, she has a home...and as you both can see, she's gone away for now. So relax!!"

The boys shake their heads and retreat inside the house. Peanut shakes her head as she watches Bali and Garam walk away angrily. Then she sits under the couch and begins to groom herself.

Peanut was practising the Fifth law of cattitude:

Treat people with empathy- that will help you win friends.

The rest of the day passes by uneventfully and the masala crew retires to bed around ten.

a true CAT stays unruffled by setbacks

Like everyday, Bali wakes up Manu at six and is rewarded by a full bowl. Manu then proceeds to fix himself breakfast. It's been a pleasant morning.. Quiet, awash with sunshine, birds chirping amongst the treetops and the whiff of fried eggs n cream is in the air. Suddenly the coffee mug slips out of Manus hands and comes crashing on the floor!!

Within a secondRosesteps out of the bedroom. "What is all that noise!!" she demands menacingly from Manu. "the neighbours had a party till late- you could sleep through all that noise- I couldn't!! I just fell asleep!!" she screams at Manu. "Why can't you keep silent!! Its fuckin 7 am!!"

Bali, garam and Peanut sense the tension.Peanut scurries under the couch while Garam sneaks out of the kitchen mumbling to himself and shaking his head, "Hmm!! It's not going to be such a good day after all!!" Bali continues to watch the events unfold from his perch on the living room window.

"The mug just slipped out of my hands!!" Manu tries to defend himself.

"I didn't drop it on purpose!!" he adds, already busy cleaning up the floor."...and please do not screw up my day early in the morning!"

"Ah!! So it's about you again"Rosecomes back with a scorn, "your day...what about MY DAY!! My night was fucked. I slept at six and now you're waking me up at seven!!"

"STOP!!" Manu screams, "please stop!! Stop complaining early in the morning!! It just fucks the day!!"

"Yes it does!!"Roseretorts, "mine is fucked already-because you can't stay quiet!"

With that she slams the door and retreats into the bedroom.

.

Ten am findsRoseworking at her desk while Manu is sulking away on the couch trying to sketch when Bali gets off the living room window and joins Manu on the couch jumping into his lap and just sits there watching what Manu is sketching. After a while he looks up at Manu and says "why did you let her anger screw up the morning!!?? You know, your morning, our morning and her morning."

Manu drops his pencil and looks at Bali who continues "she was sleepless and irritated; she shouted at you, you shouted back and she got even angrier and shouted more and that made you more angry and screwed it up even further!! You must handle the situation with a little cattitude! It's your day, your peace of mind- dont let anything or anyone disturb it."

Manu nods his head as Bali continues "If, say,Roseis angry- let her be!! Never let others emotions entrap you. Instead of reacting the same way she did, you could have simply considered the fact that she was sleepless and irritated. Instead of looking at the situation clearly, you just got sucked into her anger and irritation!! You must meditate more!!"

"Aaah!! You think you know it all, eh?" Manu looks at Bali and asks.

"Well', Bali replies "I may not know it all but I do know a few things about cattitude and this is what the sixth law of cattitude says:**don't let unexpected events rattle and disturb your peace of mind.**"

With that Bali jumps off Manu's lap and heads off into the garden.

Come noon,Roseis working on her website while Manu is writing on his pad; the sun is shining - filtering through the treetops, projecting hundreds of dots of sunshine on the ground. Manu stops writing and looks at Bali who is sitting on a tree stump close to the front porch and has just noticed a squirrel on the roof.

Bali is totally focussed on the squirrel- body close to the ground, eyes fixed on the squirrel, hips swinging gently side to side. He mentally calculates the distance between his perch and the squirrel on the edge of the roof. He must jump from the tree stump on to the gate of the porch and from there on to the roof- all in one soft motion without the squirrel noticing it. Bali prepares himself for the jump. Manu looks on, impressed by a cat's ability to focus at will.

Bali is one with the squirrel.eyes fixed on her every move, he leaps onto the gate using it as a launchpad to jump on to the squirrel on the roof and…. Ooooh!! The unlatched gate opens the moment Bali lands on it- sending him rolling on to the terrace.

Manu can't help but burst out laughing as Bali gets up immediately giving him a look and strolls back to his perch as if nothing happened. He positions himself on the tree-stump and begins to lick his paws visibly irritated by

Manu's laughter. He looks up at Manu and says "at least I tried..and why is the gate not latched!!??"

Manu continues to laugh as Bali adds "it's not fair, you know- you laughing like that...anyway, I have a squirrel to catch" with that he turns around and walks away into the garden.

This is the seventh law of cattitude:**always give your best**;. There's a lot of planning, focus and work involved and sometimes things don't turn out the way we expect them to.**A true cat doesn't let unexpected events rattle and disturb its peace of mind. It is never distracted from the goal despite multiple setbacks- it simply takes a pause and after a while gets back to the realisation of its goal.**

a CAT takes time out to relax and play

It's early evening and the sun is preparing to set . a soft glow fills the garden. Manu andRoseare having their evening coffee as they look back at the events of the day when Jeera strolls onto the front porch; Peanut, who is sitting under the couch notices Jeera walk-in and meows to Jeera who casually positions herself under the table.

"

So, how have you been?" Peanut asks Jeera "everything alright?"

"Yes!!" Jeera replies "all good...just that it gets lonely there...no one to cuddle and play with- am all alone" Jeera adds with a sigh.

"Oh come on!! You can always come here!! Manu and Roseare too cool- they love to cuddle up with cats... and beside I am here" Peanut replies "And my brothers aren't bad either , it's just that they take time to make friends"

"Thanks Peanut"Jeera responds "you are so kind!!"

Bali walks in from the garden and stops at the entrance glaring at Jeera.He eye-balls her for a few seconds and steps onto the porch. He's got a little gift for Manu andRose!!

Roselooks at Bali and lets out a cry. "Ooooh!!! What have you brought!! It's gross!!"

Manu notices the dead squirrel in Balis mouth and gets up immediately.

"Bravo!! You finally got it!! I know you wanna show-off your hunting-trophy " he addresses the cat, "but you can't bring dead animals into the house!!" Manu tells Bali.

Bali looks up at Manu with sad eyes and says "but I got a gift for you!! Don't you like squirrels? I finally caught her!!"

Bali was demonstrating the eighth law of cattitude :

always share your gifts and achievements with friends and family.

"Thank you, but we dont need dead squirrels decaying away in some corner inside the house," Manu tells Bali as he closes the door to the house.

Bali looks a bit surprised. He sees Manu close the door and begins to shift his feet wondering what to do with the squirrel. He notices the open window and walks towards it but his way is blocked byRosewho declares sternly "no hunting-trophies in the house Mr.Bali!!"

Bali freezes in his steps and looks around and thinks, "there is no way to bring the gift into the house!! They don't want it!!" He decides against trying to makeRoseand Manu accept his gift and takes the squirrel back into the garden.

The half-dead squirrel catches the attention of Peanut and Jeera who follow Bali into the garden.Bali drops the squirrel on the ground and the squirrel tries to run away but she can't get far; Bali is on her within a second-slapping the squirrel and tossing her up in the air with his paws. Peanut and Jeera see this and run towards the squirrel. Peanut manages to snatch the squirrel away and now it's her turn to toss around the dying squirrel and play with it.The game is on and soon Garam, who was not seen till now hears the commotion and pops in the garden to check what's going on.

"Aah!! It's playtime!!" Garam's eyes light up and he joins the game.

Roseis pained by the sight and walks into the house not wanting to see the squirrel being tossed around like a ball. Manu notices that the masala-crew has included Jeera into the game and smiles to himself "finally, friends!! Good for you, Jeera; now that you are accepted by Bali and Garam you are officially a member of the masala-crew!! Look honey," Manu calls out toRose"the kids have accepted Jeera finally-even letting her play with them!!"

This is the ninth law of cattitude:

Always take time out to relax and play. Playing together gives the body exercise and builds team-spirit.

An hour later, all that remains of the squirrel are a few tufts of hair. It was a good game. The cats are now relaxing on the porch while Manu andRoseprepares dinner.

"I hope they have finished playing with the squirrel,"Rosesays while chopping the tomatoes.

"Oh yes" Manu replies, " I am sure they have!! It was funny...how he brought the squirrel in," Manu giggles.

"Ugh!! It's gross!!"Rosereplies "I've had enough of dead lizards, dead frogs and dead squirrels in the house"

"I know" Manu answers defensively "it's just that a few hours before Bali was trying to catch the squirrel and fell on the ground so naturally I was happy to see the kid succeed finally"

"You and your kids"Rosereplies "now handle this kid" she adds pointing towards Garam who is at her feet rubbing himself against her legs.

Manu sees Garam and immediately chides him "not in the kitchen Garam!!"

Garam quietly walks out of the kitchen back to the porch waiting patiently for his dinner. Soon, dinner is served. Manu andRosefinish off the meal and notice the cats eating together from the same bowl; they both smile and retire to the bedroom joined by Peanut.

"Ah!! Finally we can rest"Rosesighs as she turns off the light.

a true CAT knows to move on and keeps learning

It's been raining all night and Manu wakes up a little late at around 6:30. He sits up in the bed and wonders rubbing his eyes "strange!! Bali is not up!!" He then gets out of the bedroom, gets ready for the day and puts milk in the bowl for the cats.

"Good morning kitties!! Breakfast time!" Manu calls out as he places the bowl on the porch and waits. One by one, Garam,Peanut and Jeera show up. Bali continues to sleep on the couch, merely opening his eyes and looking at Manu who walks over to him and picks him up in his arms.

"What's up Mr.fluffy??" Manu asks Bali. "You didn't even wake me up and now you just sleep!! Don't you feel like having breakfast?"

Bali looks up at Manu with sad eyes and puts his head down again. Manu puts him back on the couch and goes into the house talking to himself, "hmmm..rain all night so the cats can't go out; maybe that's why Bali is depressed."

It's a rain soaked day and things don't move much. Manu spends most of the day writing Bali sitting in his lap while Anika is busy with her coaching and yoga. It's a "gonna stay in bed" day for Peanut while Garam stays put on the couch with Jeera cuddled under it. Around sunset while feeding the kids Manu notices Bali not eating much and points this out toRosewho says that he is also moving slow and lethargic. "Well, look at the weather," they both say in unison "even we feel lethargic and slow!"

That evening Manu andRosedecided to go to bed early. It was a slow and long dark rainy day!! Peanut as usual comfortably in her bed and Garam out in the garden; Bali simply crawled into the bed with Manu who tucked him by his side.

"Aw! Little Bali, u feel sad!!" Manu says as he scratches Balis head "I know- rain all day, no sun, can't really step out...it's been a tiring day but tomorrow will be wonderful!! For now,you can sleep with papa"

Bali opens his eyes slightly to look at Manu and begins to purr…

The next morning too, Manu wakes up without Bali.Still cold and wet outside from the night's rain, the garden glows softly in the early-morning light. Manu freshens up and fills up the kitty bowl. And one by one the cats join-in ; crawling out of their beds, stretching themselves and greeting Manu with a "meow" before proceeding for breakfast. Bali is the last one to show up- he walks really slow and doesn't look alright.Manu is a bit worried and ponders over taking Bali to the vet and decides to do that during the day.

Around eight, while having their breakfast on the porch, Manu andRosewatch Bali as he crawls up on the couch.

"He is really slow,"Roseremarks. "I think we should take him to the vet- he always jumps on the couch but today its as if he has no strength."

 "Yes, I shall take him there right now," Manu answers "was thinking to do it in the evening but no- he doesn't look good"

Half an hour later Manu is at the veterinarian's clinic with Bali.

"It's a good thing you brought him here," the vet tells Manu, "looks like cat-flu. I shall give him a shot now and we shall see how he fares till tomorrow. Ideally he should be ok by morning; if his condition doesn't improve please bring him back to me!"

Manu gives thanks to the doctor. And returns home with advice to keep .Bali indoors till he gets ok.

"So what did the doctor say?"Rosedemands.

"Cat-flu!!" Manu answers " the doctor said it's good we got to the clinic. He gave him an injection saying it should be ok till morning. If not, we have to visit him again.we have to keep him inside till hes ok"

"Ok! I shall arrange a spot for him in the second bedroom"Rosesays as she gets up and heads to the second bedroom.

Within minutes Bali is tucked in his bed. He doesn't move much and opens his eyes weakly to look atRosewho is talking to him in whispers, "it will be all ok Mr.Bali!! By morning you will be running around in the garden!"

The following morning Manu woke up to find Bali gone.Manu had forgotten to close the window!! He gets out of the bed quickly, freshens up and then fills the kitty bowl for breakfast...Garam, Jeera and Peanut show up but Bali is not to be seen. Manu calls out a few times for Bali and then concludes that Bali must have recovered and has gone out to the neighbours garden. At around seven Manu begins to look for Bali in the garden. After fifteen minutes or so he finds him lying in a pit, wimping unable to move.Manu quickly grabs Bali and brings him in. Balii doesn't look alright!!

In about twenty minutes he is at the vet's who looks at Bali and says,"it doesn't look good. We give him something to stabilize his condition. Once he is stable, we can treat him further."

The vet administers a vaccine and then Bali is hooked on a drip to hydrate his body. Sadly, nothing seems to help little Bali and soon he starts getting fits. His tiny body jerks in spasms as his brain begins to shut down. He wants to run out and is crying loud. Manu tries to soothe him, talking softly.

After a while the doctor walks over, takes a look at Balis eyes and mouth then turns around and tells Manu,"I am sorry but we will have to put him to sleep. His condition is not improving."

"Is there no way to save him?" Manu asks, choking on his own words "please doctor!! He is my baby!!"

"I am sorry" the doctor says, "we need you to fill this form before we put him to sleep".

Manu is in a state of shock and is looking at the form. His eyes fall on the column marked "date of birth" and he begins to cry. It's Balis first birthday today!!

The doctor looks at Manu and asks "you have filled it?"

"I can't!!" Manu replies with tears in his eyes, "it's his birthday!! How can I put him to sleep?"

"Look", the doctor puts his hand on Manus shoulder and replies, "we have done all we could!! There is no way to save him...his body is dehydrated and his liver has stopped functioning turning his blood toxic. He is dying and there's nothing we can do about it!! The least we can do to make it easier for him to leave this world peacefully and without any pain is to put him to sleep. Believe me, he will have a painful death if we just let him be."

Tears run down Manus cheeks as he fills in the form...he hesitates before signing it. He holds Balis jerking body down with his hands and tries to caress him gently, trying in vain to hold his tears back as the doctor fills up the syringe and gives Bali the shot.

"Ten minutes and he will be asleep forever" the doctor tells him.

Manu begins to cry out loud, holding Bali close to his chest, telling him how much he and Anika love him and how sorry they are to see him go. Someone hands him tissues to wipe his face. Manu grabs it and continues to cry.. Holding Bali in his arms,watching him relax and die...his little body becoming heavy and limp in his arms. He sits down on a chair in the clinic and waits for Bali to breathe his last...still talking to him softly, wishing him the final farewell.

Manu reached home with Bali andRoserushed out to meet them. She saw that sad look on his face and she knew Bali was gone.

Little Bali now rests in the back garden under the shade of Banana and mango trees.

Manu andRosewere deeply saddened by Bali's death and so were the rest of the masala-crew.Peanut and Garam spent the morning after Balis burial at his grave...for days, they would wait for a while and look over their shoulders if Bali was coming to join them in eating food. It was sad to see this...little by little in a few weeks the sadness was gone and the masala-crew learnt to move on after the loss.

Almost a month had passed by since Bali's death when one day, while out at the post-office,Roseheard the cries of a kitten- wailing non-stop. She asked the woman at the desk where this sound was coming from?

"Oh, a cat gave birth to a litter in our old storage...the mother has not returned since last night and so the baby is crying…"

"Where's it?"Rosecut the woman mid sentence.

"You step out and go to the backside of this building. There's and open door- that's the old storage we have abandoned"

Roserushed out quickly. She entered the door and found herself in a dark abandoned storage space- the only source of light was a dusty old glass window. There were old telephones and boxes lying around.Empty beer bottles and broken glass lay all over the floor.Rosetiptoed in the dark - the kitten was still crying out loud.

"Hello kitty!!",Rosecalled out in the dark, "where are you, little one?"

The kitten called out again andRosewalked towards the sound in the dimly lit room. She found it behind an office table standing in one corner, lying on the floor amidst old rags and paper. There was no sign of any other kitten around.Rosefound that strange as cats usually give birth to a litter. "Maybe the others died", she thought. She bent down and picked up the kitten and immediately it stopped crying. It looked straight into her eyes andRosecouldn't help but smile...seen in the dark was the face of a tiny kitten, black patches around her eyes exactly like little Bali. She knew it right then that she would adopt this kitten.

"What!! Another kitten!!", Manu exclaimed the momentRosewalked in.

"It was abandoned by the mother..found him at the post office...he's been crying since last night- alone in the dark;

the moment I picked him up, it stopped crying. look at his face!!"Roseheld up the kitten to Manu, "doesn't he look like little Bali??! He must be a month old...born at the same time as Balis death...I feel our Bali has come back!!"

Manu just smiled at her and nodded a yes as he took the little kitten in his hands.

"What shall we call her??" he askedRose.

"I don't know... let me think,Rosesaid scratching her head, "Coco!! How about Coco?? Sounds elegant ...like CocoChanel..and Coco-Masala has a nice ring to it."

Manu just looked atRoseand smiled.

"One more cat!! Wonder how many new lessons to learn", he thought.

CATtitude is about courage, persistance and friendships

The coming of CocoMasala cleared the heaviness in the house left because of Bali's death. The tiny thing was really grateful to be rescued - happy to find herself in a warm place with her own tiny bed. She slept in her bed and always woke up early- waiting till Manu andRosewoke up- greeting them with her wide eyes shining, a surprised expression on her face. No sooner that the couple woke up, Coco would jump out of her bed and start to run around their feet.

Garam and Peanut masala were not so happy about her arrival though. The first day Coco was brought into the house, Garam (the sensitive one) noticed the closed door to the room where CocoMasala was kept.

"I smell a cat!! A stranger!!," he exclaimed and looked atRosewith wide eyes.

Roseunderstood Garam's feelings and tried to explain to him the whole situation- how she found this little baby abandoned and that they had to save her!! Garams's eyes widened even more on hearing her story.

"I can't believe you can do this!!" he said, "I mean ...this is OUR house and before you make a decision, you have to ask us too!!" He looked atRose, a bewildered look on his face.

"It's ok Garam,"Rosepicked him up and tried to make him understand, "you too, were once a tiny baby and needed your mother to take care of you; this one has no mother or any brothers and sisters!! Coco would have died if I had left her there." she said.

Garam wouldn't have none of it!! He growled and jumped out of her arms and walked out into the garden. Peanut's reaction was similar to Garam. She entered the house and froze in her place, sniffing the air. After a brief moment she simply walked out talking to herself, " I just don't like too many changes!!"

The couple realised that they had a problem at hand. The old masala crew would take time to accept Coco into the family. A plan was made to introduce Coco bit by bit to the crew. She would share the bedroom with them-her tiny bed covered with a piece of cloth; after a few days that piece of cloth would be taken out and put near Garam and Peanuts place on the front porch so that they get used to Coco's smell and a few more days later all of the cats would be brought face to face.

Coco was introduced to the other parts of the house after three days and one could see her excitement. Her eyes were all lit up and she ran from one corner to another soaking-in new smells and textures. She explored every nook and cranny of the house: under the bed, behind the wardrobe, under the kitchen sink and around the table in the library. She paused for a long time sniffing the couch. One could tell that she had sensed the presence of other cats in the house. She had her first encounter with the masala-crew around noon when Garam and Peanut walked into the house for lunch.

The moment she saw them, Coco was excited!! She hid behind a curtain and watched Garam and Peanut walk in. Once both of them started eating, Coco stepped out from behind the curtain and exposed herself. Immediately Garam started to growl and hiss at Coco. Coco approached Garam with caution, body pressed close to the floor, eyes fixed on Garam and a friendly expression on her face. Garam saw Coco approach and he just turned around and vanished into the garden with a growl. Peanut didn't even wait for Coco to approach her. One could see that she didn't know how to react to the tiny one- she too, walked away into the garden.

Evening came and the same thing was repeated during dinner. Peanut even refused to sleep in her bed at night!!She could smell the new cat all over the house!! When Manu picked her up and put her in the bed, she protested and looked at Manu, "I am NOT sharing my bed with another strange cat", she said as she jumped out of the window.

It was a serious issue. The rainy season was on and it rained heavily everyday;Roseand Manu were sad to see their beloved Garam masala and Peanut masala sort of abandoning the house and sleeping out somewhere else. Everyday the older kids would drop in for the meals and then walk away from the house: they had made themselves comfortable inside an unfinished construction just outside the house. Manu andRosewere saddened to see their beloved cats sleep out on the floor with no protection from the wind.

"Don't worry,love", Manu toldRose, "I read about introducing a new cat to your pet cats.it takes them three to four weeks to accept a new member in the family."

"I know"Rosereplied, "they will take time. Especially Garam- he is the boss and now he sees Coco as someone taking over his empire"

Coco continued her efforts towards making friends with Garam n Peanut. The little soul was so full of innocence and positivity that she didn't mind being shunned by the older cats- even after getting slapped by Garam a couple of times, she continued to approach him full of enthusiasm, wanting to play.

Coco was demonstrating**the tenth law of cattitude: approach life full of courage! Even if you get "slapped around" by life, persist in your endeavours and you shall have a breakthrough!**

:

One afternoon Garam walked in the living room to find little Coco sleeping on Manu's lap. Garam stopped in his tracks and first looked at Manu then Coco- his eyes widening in surprise!!

"Hmmmm!! Now she gets all the cuddles!!", he glared at Manu,"how can you!!?? We are the masala-crew!! I get to sit on your lap and get cuddles!! NOT this kid!!"

"It's ok, Garam", Manu tried to reason with Garam,"it's a small baby- just like you were a year before- you were lucky to have a mom and brothers and sisters; this one is alone and that's why we brought her home.Look, she wants to make friends and play with you !!"

Garam just stood rooted to the spot staring at Coco masala sleeping on Manu's lap. He tried to understand the situation as he stood there for a long time just looking at Coco- eyes wide, jealousy on his face until Manu called

Garam to join him on the couch. He simply turned around and walked away.

The breakthrough came after three weeks. It was noon and Garam was having lunch on the front porch; Peanut by now had started eating up on the porch wall (the tiny one could climb up till now). Halfway through lunch, Coco stepped on the porch after finishing her bowl and hid behind a couch leg- observing Garam- trying to gauge his mood. Garam, still busy eating, didn't notice Coco approaching from behind.

Roseand Manu looked on with excitement. Little Coco stepped out gingerly, crawling towards Garam. His tail swaying from side to side caught Coco's attention and when she was close enough, she raised a paw to touch Garam's tail. She held back for a while, her paw shaking with excitement to touch Garam's tail, her eyes fixed on it as it swayed from side to side..and then she touched it!! Immediately, Garam turned around and looked at Coco, who had retreated a few steps back after making contact. They both stood transfixed- looking at each other.

"You little brat!!"Garam addressed Coco, "I am Garam masala: head of the masala crew!! Nobody messes with me...and I have no interest in you childish games. Stay away!!", he hissed.

Coco retreated further under the couch without taking her eyes off Garam, "Hello... I...I am Coco masala and I would like to make friends with you!!" she spoke to Garam, "why don't we play!! It's so much fun!!"

Garam simply growled at her and continued eating. Coco climbed up on the table and watched Garam eat under it- her little paws reaching out to tease Garam who looked up at her a couple of times with a bewildered expression. He finished lunch and climbed up the porch wall taking a place next to Peanut; both of them looking at Coco. The three of them sat where they were for a while, giving each other glances.

"Ah!! Finally they sit close to each other!!",Roseclapped her hands and looked at Manu, "at least now they don't run away!! Am sure soon they will be playing together!!". she was excited.

She picked up Coco and took her in the house, wanting to let Garam and Peanut stay undisturbed for a while. Garam noticedRosetake the little one inside the house- his eyes followingRoseuntil she closed the bedroom door. He then got off his perch and walked up to the bedroom door- pausing a few steps away from it.He stood there staring at the door, the wheels inside his brain moving. Manu looked at him and chuckled. He could see that Garam was trying to digest the fact that the little one was now a part of the family and that they would have to share the house, the food and their slaves. Garam turned his head to look at Manu when he heard him chuckle and jumped into Manu's lap.

"Hey Mr.Garam!!"Manu spoke as he scratched Garam's head, "You see, Coco is a part of the masala-crew now...new addition but it doesn't mean we love you less!!". He grabbed Garam's paws and kissed it. "You are still my little Garam!! And we love you too!!", he said looking at Garam in the eyes. Garam closed his eyes and started to purr as Manu continued to massage him- the top of the head first then under the chin and then a belly rub. That's what Garam likes.

That evening, Garam treated Coco differently. He still refused to play with her but was tolerant of the little one playing with his tail. Princess peanut chose to maintain distance from the little one.

Then one day, garam allows her to eat out of his bowland and joins Coco for siesta at noon. :)

Finally, the complete masala-crew eating together!!

This demonstrated**the eleventh law of cattitude: Make all efforts to have friends in your life; life is pleasant with friends.**

Try and make friends: even with your perceived enemies!